THE ADVENTURES OF
Daisy & Tom

THE RAINBOW

Story by Rosie Alison

Pictures by Atholl McDonald

For Oliver Rudd: R.A.

First published in Great Britain in 2003 by
The Rose Press, Daisy and Tom, Granville House,
2a Pond Place, London SW3 6QJ

Reprinted 2006

Copyright © Text Rosie Alison
Illustrations by Atholl McDonald

The moral right of the author has been asserted

ISBN: 1 - 901503 - 01 -1

Manufactured in China by Imago

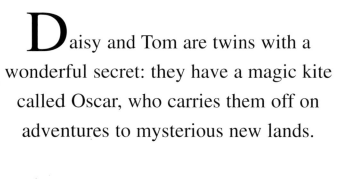

Daisy and Tom are twins with a wonderful secret: they have a magic kite called Oscar, who carries them off on adventures to mysterious new lands.

Time and again they fly off together, knowing that Oscar will always bring them safely back home in the end.

It was a wet morning and Daisy and Tom were stuck indoors watching the *drip-drip-drip* of the rain. Both of them felt glum. But as they watched and waited, a sunburst suddenly parted the clouds and a rainbow unrolled across the sky ...

The twins knew the story about a crock of gold at the end of every rainbow, and here was their chance to find it. Quickly they ran out into the garden with their magic kite.

"Follow that rainbow, please Oscar!" they asked, and away they went, up into the sky.

The rainbow *seemed* to be close but it was far away. Oscar carried them as fast as he could, trying to catch the rainbow before it vanished. They swooped deep into valleys and high over hills until at last they reached the great arch of the rainbow itself ...

How high it was, and soft, and bouncy. Daisy and Tom
clambered all over the different colours, and jumped
up and down until they were dizzy. Then, tired out,
they lay on their backs and gazed up at the sky.
What a place to rest, on a rainbow's back!

But after a while they were ready to look for the crock of gold – so down they went, sliding all the way to the ground ...

To their surprise, they found the rainbow's end tied by ropes to a large balloon basket. Nearby was a gathering of small people, all wearing rainbow hats. In the middle of the group the twins were astonished to see their old friend Mr Whistlewind – whom they had met on an earlier adventure in the Kingdom of the Sun.

"Daisy and Tom – and Oscar!" called Mr Whistlewind, as they landed.

The twins were warmly welcomed but nobody could hide that something was wrong.

"This is the Rainbow Family," explained Mr Whistlewind, "who set up a rainbow wherever there's rain and sunshine. But they have a problem: their famous crock of gold has been stolen, and they can't fly off without it."

Father Rainbow explained that his son Sparky had hidden the treasure behind a tree whilst he was cleaning the crock ...

Sparky polished the crock till it gleamed, then reached over to put the treasure back inside – but it had all vanished!

He saw someone disappear down the river bank, so he ran after him – but too late, the thief had already gone ...

Eager to help, Daisy and Tom followed Sparky over to the river bank and they all looked for some sign of the treasure thief. They climbed along the bank until they reached a waterfall which tumbled down into a deep pool with stepping stones. But there was no sign of anything unusual.

Just then, they had a bit of luck. There was a sudden gust of wind and Oscar went flying towards the waterfall.

"Hold on!" called Daisy to Tom, who stood his ground as Oscar dived into the water. But when Tom tried to reel Oscar in again, the kite seemed to be stuck. "He must be caught on something behind the waterfall," said Tom.

But Daisy had another idea.

"I think Oscar is showing us a way *through* the waterfall," she said. She hopped down onto the stepping stones and clambered along the string. Quickly, she disappeared behind a wall of water.

Tom and Sparky followed at once, with Mr Whistlewind close behind. They came through to find Daisy and Oscar shaking off water in a dimly lit cave. Beyond them was a small green mining truck leading into a dark tunnel.

"Come on!" whispered Daisy, "this must be the way."

W*hoosh!* They held onto each other as the truck went rushing down steep tracks deep into the mountainside ...

They landed with a bump in a vast echoing cave where a brilliant treasure hoard glowed in the dim light.

"There's the rainbow gold!" cried Sparky.

But before they could blink, a strange creature leapt forward and grabbed the treasure, scuttling off into another tunnel.

"It's a water troll!" exclaimed Mr Whistlewind.

"Is he dangerous?" asked Tom.

"No, but they're very shy, so we must go carefully."

They split up and set off down different tunnels.

Daisy glimpsed the
water troll running
round a corner ...

Tom and Sparky chased
him through a tunnel ...

... Then Mr Whistlewind finally
cornered him in the big cavern ...

"Don't be afraid!" said Daisy gently. "We've only come to take back the rainbow gold – you may not have realised what you were taking." The water troll looked up at her, and she saw at once how shy and scared he was.

"I'm sorry," he said in a small voice. "I'm stuck here underground, and I long for things to brighten my darkness. So when I saw the treasure, I couldn't resist the sparkle."

"But why do you have to stay down here?" asked Tom.

"Because I'm afraid," said the troll sadly. "If I show my face in the open air somebody might catch me and put me in a zoo. So I have to stay in hiding – but really, I long to live in the sun."

"Do you by any chance like gardening?" chipped in Mr Whistlewind.

"Of course – but that pleasure is hardly possible for me."

"Well, I think you could help me out," he went on. "My neighbour in the Sun Kingdom has gone to live with her daughter. She's left behind an empty treehouse – and below it, a fine tulip garden that needs far more care than I can manage. She wanted me to tend it, but frankly, I'd rather you did – "

The troll's face creased into a happy smile. He could hardly believe his luck. And as soon as he smiled, he no longer looked frightening.

"Are you sure?" he asked. "Quite sure," came the reply.

"Then please – take back your treasure!" said the troll, and he skipped off to pack.

The troll reappeared with a small suitcase, then
they all clambered back into the truck with
the gold. Mr Whistlewind blew with his
great cheeks so that Oscar could pull them
all the way back up to the waterfall.

They plunged back through the wall of water,
blinking in the sunshine and shaking themselves dry. The troll
felt shy and scared to be seen in the clear light of day, so Daisy
gently took his hand.

The Rainbow family greeted them all with joy and thanks. At last they were ready to haul the rainbow back into its basket, and fly off to their next calling. Sparky climbed aboard, proudly holding onto the crock of gold. He waved off his new friends.

"See you again another day!" he cried, as the balloon began to rise ...

"Next stop the Sun Kingdom!" announced Mr Whistlewind. He led the twins and the troll over to his magic boat (Oscar, for once, could have a rest.) He whistled up a wind and they all set sail through the sky to the Kingdom of the Sun ...

They flew past the spires of the Sun King's palace and came to rest in a grove of treehouses.

"Welcome to your new home!" cried Mr Whistlewind. There were tears of joy in the troll's eyes. He could hardly believe his luck: he had been released from a dark cave into this magical sunlit land ...

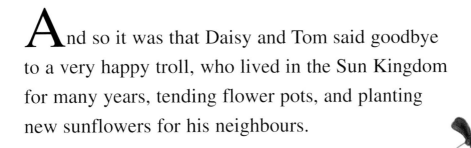

And so it was that Daisy and Tom said goodbye to a very happy troll, who lived in the Sun Kingdom for many years, tending flower pots, and planting new sunflowers for his neighbours.

"Come and visit us again soon!" called Mr Whistlewind, as the twins at last began their journey home with Oscar.

Flying back to earth, they could see their rickety hillside house below. Oscar carried them quietly down to the ground, careful not to give away their flying secret. There, in the garden, their mother was painting a picture ...

They might have guessed it would be a rainbow ...